COCK-A-DOODLE-DOO

COCK-A-DOODLE DOO

THE STORY OF A LITTLE RED ROOSTER by BERTA and ELMER HADER

THE MACMILLAN CO. NEW YORK

Published October, 1939
Reprinted October, 1940
Reprinted September, 1941
Reprinted September, 1943
Reprinted July, 1944
Reprinted April, 1945

LITHOGRAPHED IN THE UNITED STATES
BY THE DUENEWALD PRINTING CORPORATION

AFFECTIONATELY
DEDICATED TO
LITTLE CHUCK

COCK-A-DOODLE-DOO
The Story of a Little Red Rooster

"Quack," said the big ducks. "Quack," said the little ducks. "Quack-quack," said all the ducks together. They made a great noise on the farm beside the pond. It was spring and there were many pools in the marshy farmland. The ducks swam in the pools and ate the tender water greens. It was a wonderful place for ducks.

One day a newcomer poked a downy head out of his shell. "Peep-peep," he said.

That was very strange, for no duckling had ever said "Peep-peep" before. The old mother duck and the six yellow ducklings stared at him. His beak was short and pointed. His feet were not webbed and his coat was a rusty red. He was not a duckling at all! He was A LITTLE RED CHICK! The old mother duck was surprised, but she took the baby chick under her wing with the ducklings.

The farmer was surprised, too. "Oh well," he said, "he will get along all right with the ducks." He put some mash in the trough and went away.

One day the old mother duck led her family down the hill to the pond. The little red chick followed the others.

"Quack-quack," said the mother duck as she swam out on the pond. The ducklings swam right after her.

The little red chick stepped into the water. "Peep-peep," he said and he stepped right out again. He could not swim and he did not like to get wet.

He shook himself dry and waited for his family to come out of the water. "Peep-peep," he called sadly.

Every day the little red chick followed the ducklings to the pond; but he could not swim like a duck nor quack like a duck, and he grew more and more lonely.

Then one morning he heard a call from the other side of the hill.

"Cock-a-doodle-doo. Come home, come home, wherever you are."

The little red chick understood that call. He decided to go to the farm on the top of the hill. He flapped his tiny wings and tried very hard to fly over the fence around the yard.

But the fence was too high, so he hunted until he found an opening just big enough to squeeze through.

"Come back," quacked the ducklings. "There are wild animals in the woods and they will catch you."

The little red chick did not understand. He looked at the wide meadow and the woods beyond but he did not turn back. He was FREE and he was not afraid. He hurried across the road and ran into the meadow.

"Caw-caw!" cried a big black crow from a branch of a dogwood tree. He was watching a sparrow on her nest.

"Peep-peep!" said Little Red and he quickly hid in the tall grass. He was glad the crow had not seen him.

"Caw-caw-caw!" The old crow forgot the nest he was going to rob when he heard the "peep-peep" of a little chick. He cocked his head to one side and then the other. He tried to see Little Red in the grass.

The little chick kept very quiet until the crow flew away. Then he ran on through the meadow.

It was dark when Little Red came to the woods. He hopped under a bayberry bush to spend the night. A big owl flew silently to the branch of a hemlock near by.

"Whooooooooooooooooooo," called the owl, and every downy hair on Little Red's head stood on end. He was sure the owl was *not* a friend and he kept very quiet.

A wood mouse ran along the path. He did not see the owl in the tree, but the owl saw him and a mouse was just what he wanted for dinner.

"PEEP-PEEP!" cried Little Red as loud as he could. That cry warned the mouse and he darted under a moss-covered log. And just in time, too.

"Whoooooooooooooooooooooooo," screeched the owl, angrily and he looked hard for Little Red. But the little chick did not move, and after a while the owl flew away.

Then Little Red went to sleep. He was awakened by a skunk who passed at midnight and a big raccoon at dawn. But they did not see him, which was very lucky for Little Red.

"Cock-a-doodle-doo. Come home, come home, wher-ever you are." The call of the cock from over the hill woke Little Red. He hopped from under the bayberry bush and hurried through the woods.

"Chet-chet-chet-chet-chet!" Three gray squirrels in a birch tree nearby barked their warning of danger ahead.

Little Red looked at the squirrels but he did not understand what they were saying. "Peep-peep," he said and he continued on his way.

Then he saw the FOX! "PEEP-PEEP!" cried Little Red

and he ran as fast as he could to get out of the woods.

"PEEP!" cried the frightened Little Red as he passed a chipmunk sitting in the sun.

With a whisk of his tail, the chipmunk turned and disappeared behind a rock.

"PEEP!" cried Little Red again, as he came to a baby rabbit nibbling clover.

Quick as a wink, the rabbit dived into his home underground.

Little Red's heart beat very fast as he scrambled to hide under the leaves.

The fox leaped through the brush. He was hungry and a fat little chick would make a nice breakfast. He sniffed here and he sniffed there, and with each sniff he drew closer to Little Red.

"BOW-WOW-WOW-OOooooooooooo!" The dogs from the farm over the hill had smelled the fox. They bounded into the woods.

The fox forgot all about Little Red and ran for his life, with the barking dogs close behind him. And Little Red ran out of the woods and over the hill.

"Here, chick. Here, chick. Chick-chick-chick-chick."
Little Red stopped and looked toward a big red barn.
He lifted his head and listened.

"Kut-kut-kadawkut," cackled some snow-white hens.
"Kut-kut-kadawkut! Hurry, hurry—it's time to eat."
And they ran into the barnyard.

"Peep-peep!" cried Little Red happily. That was a
call he could understand, and he ran after the hens.

"Gobble-gobble-gobble," cried three big turkeys.

"Honk-honk-honk." Three fat geese waddled by and
followed the turkeys into the chicken yard.

"Here, chick. Here, chick. Chick, chick, chick," called

a little girl as she threw handfuls of grain on the
ground. Then she went into the barn.

The turkeys ate fast. The chickens ate faster.

The geese ate as fast as they could. But just as Little

Red ran into the yard a shadow passed over the ground. The watchful guinea hen looked at the sky.

"Scrammmmmmmmmmm!" she screamed. "Run, chicks! Run!"

Little Red looked up at the sky and he, too, saw the HAWK!

"Peep-peep!" he cried, and he ran after the chickens.

The three big turkeys ran into the barn.

The three fat geese waddled to their shed.

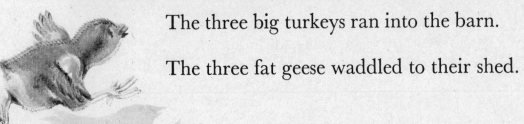

The snow-white chickens pushed and shoved their way into the henhouse. Poor Little Red ran as fast as he could, but he was very little and the hawk was very near.

The hawk opened his claws to grab the little chick.

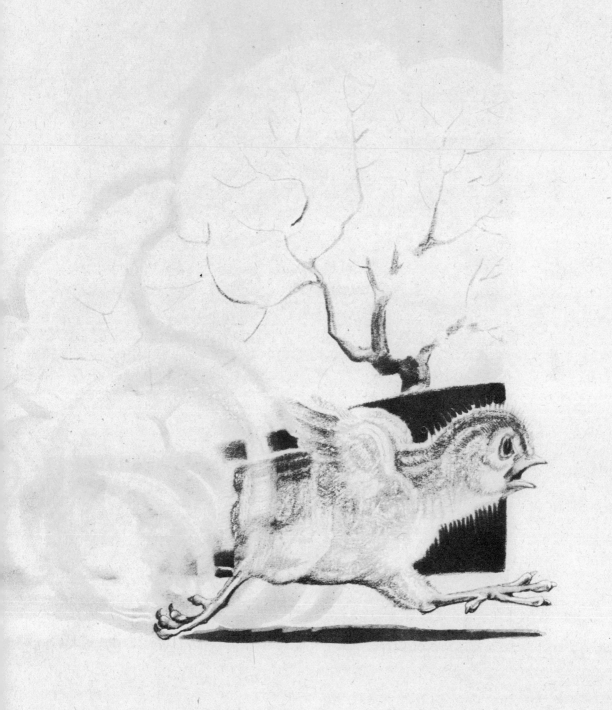

"Peep-peep," cried Little Red as he dashed through the door into the chicken house. He was safe. The big hawk flew away.

"Peep-peep-peep-peep-peep-peep," chirped a whole family of yellow chicks as they hopped from under their mother's wing and looked at the newcomer.

Little Red was filled with joy to see chicks just like himself. He knew he would be very happy here.

"Cock-a-doodle-dooooooo!"

Little Red ran into the yard when the cock crowed.

The snow-white cock flapped his wings and sang: "Cock-a-doodle-dooooooooooooooooooooooooo!"

"Honk-honk," said the geese. "Gobble-gobble," said the turkeys. "Kut-kut-kadawcut," called the chickens.

The warm sun shone on the apple blossoms and underneath the trees the chicken yard was dry and dusty. The chickens were back again eating cracked wheat and corn. It was a WONDERFUL place for chickens, and Little Red was home at last.

Red rose early every morn;
   He ate wheat and grubs and corn.

He grew fast and he grew tall;
   Summer passed, and then came fall.

He grew a tail of brightest red
   And wore a comb upon his head.

Now Red gets up at break of day,
   And this is what he has to say:

"Get up, get up, there's work for you.
Cock-a-doodle-doodle-doo."

BY BERTA AND ELMER HADER

Cricket

Spunky

Midget and Bridget

Billy Butter

Jamaica Johnny

Tommy Thatcher Goes to Sea

Green and Gold: The Story of the Banana

The Farmer in the Dell

The Picture Book of Travel